DOG DIARIES

FIDO

DOG DIARIES

DOG DIARIES

FIDO

BY KATE KLIMO • ILLUSTRATED BY TIM JESSELL

RANDOM HOUSE 🏠 NEW YORK

The author and editor would like to thank James M. Cornelius, PhD, curator,
Lincoln Collection, Abraham Lincoln Presidential Library and Museum, Springfield, Illinois,
for his assistance in the preparation of this book.

Visit us on the Web! rhcbooks.com

Educators and librarians, for a variety of teaching tools, visit us at
RHTeachersLibrarians.com

Library of Congress Cataloging-in-Publication Data
Names: Klimo, Kate, author. | Jessell, Tim, illustrator.
Title: Fido / by Kate Klimo ; illustrated by Tim Jessell.
Description: First edition. | New York : Random House, 2018. | Series: Dog
diaries | Audience: Age: 7–10.
Identifiers: LCCN 2017030222 (print) | LCCN 2017032926 (ebook) |
ISBN 978-1-5247-1967-8 (trade) | ISBN 978-1-5247-1968-5 (lib. bdg.) |
ISBN 978-1-5247-1969-2 (ebook)
Subjects: LCSH: Lincoln, Abraham, 1809–1865—Juvenile literature. | Fido (Dog),
1855–1866—Juvenile literature. | Presidents' pets—United States—History—19th century—
Juvenile literature. | Dogs—United States—Biography—Juvenile literature. | Human-animal
relationships—United States—History—19th century—Juvenile literature.
Classification: LCC E457.25 (ebook) | LCC E457.25 .K55 2018 (print) |
DDC 973.7092—dc23

Printed in the United States of America

10 9 8 7 6 5 4 3 2 1

First Edition

For Cody, one magnificent mutt

—K.K.

For dogs, who are as truthful as Honest Abe

—T.J.

Contents

Abraham Lincoln in 1857, immediately before his Senate nomination

A Little Yaller Pup

Abraham Lincoln was my man and I was his dog. That's the long and short of it. Lincoln had lots of dogs. This ain't about them. This is about me, Fido. I like to think I was his favorite. The Lincoln Dog, they called me in my heyday. But before I met him, I waren't nothing but a tramp, living on the streets.

Fact is, me and Lincoln looked alike. We were, the both of us, raw-boned and big-eared and, if

I do say so myself, homely as the day is long.

The morning we met, I'd been trussed up tight in a burlap sack, captured by a gang of ne'er-do-well boys. I didn't know what they had in mind for me. But I can tell you right now, it waren't good. I could tell by the sound of their wicked laughter. Low-down and mean it was.

I'd no one to blame but myself. They'd lured me into an alleyway with the promise of bacon. I should've known better. My mother would have told me, *Son, when you see a band of idle boys coming at you, run in t'other direction.* But Ma was gone, squashed flatter than a johnnycake by a lumber wagon. Before I could get me my taste of bacon, those bad boys had me in a feed sack with the string drawed up tight, quicker than greased lightning.

Let me go! I barked till my jaws ached.

Suddenly, I heard a voice. It was high and

twangy, like a country banjo. "What are you boys proposing to do with that there wriggling sack?"

The boys knocked off laughing. I heard them shuffle and mumble. "Bringin' home a rooster for Ma's cook pot," one of them said.

"Is that a fact?" said the man. "Rare rooster you've got there that barks like a dog."

"Boys," I heard one of them whispering to another, "we're in hot water now."

The man went on. "Don't you young 'uns know that all life is sacred? An ant's life is as sweet to it as ours is to us. How would you like it if somebody stuffed you in a sack?"

"I reckon we'd hate it, sir," one of the boys said.

"Then you'd best drop that sack and be off. And the next time I catch you red-handed, I'll tell your folks. And if they don't tan your hide, I will. Hear me?"

"Yes, sir, mister!" And they dropped me.

Next thing I knew, the man was laying open the sack. He squatted on his heels and stared down at me. I was shivering so bad I thought my teeth would crack. In my brief life on earth, humans had done precious little to win my trust. I looked in this one's eyes. They were pale as a rainy day. He smelled of timber, woodsmoke, river, milk, barn, and what else? I took a deeper whiff. Sadness! He smelled like a man weighed down by a great sadness.

I leapt into his lap. Propping my paws on his chest, I wagged my bushy tail. *Cheer up!*

Some dogs might have been afeared of his looks. His face was long and narrow, with sunken cheeks. His hat was tall and dusty. But that smile? It lit up his face like a lantern in the wilderness.

"I've found me a little yaller pup, looks like!" he

declared, scratching my back. "A good little dog, too, I can tell."

Even a tramp like me knew that word. *Good*. But was I anything like good? I knew I *wanted* to be. Ma always *told* me to be. But she also said there waren't nothing like a man to bring out the best in a dog. Was this the man for me?

I licked his face until he laughed so hard he fell over backward. "I know some fine young lads who will be pleased to meet you."

He climbed to his feet and wrapped me in the old shawl from around his neck. It smelled of man sweat and hair oil. Down the street he strode on legs so long I got dizzy when I looked down.

We passed a lady coming t'other way. The man tipped his tall hat. "Good day, Mrs. Melvin."

The lady stopped and grinned. "Well, now, I see you've rescued another of God's creatures."

"Now, Mother Melvin, you know I can't help myself."

The lady shook her head fondly. "Aren't you the one who ruined a brand-new suit wading into the mud to save a pig in distress?"

"I do confess I'm partial to pigs, ma'am. My favorite pet as a child was a pig. But I favor little yaller dogs, too."

"I wonder what your Mary will have to say about that," Mother Melvin said. "Cats she'll tolerate. But everyone knows the little woman is afeared of dogs. I daresay she'll be fit to be tied."

"Over a little yaller pup?" He looked down on me, his eyes twinkling. "What say you, Fido?"

I wagged and panted. *Fido? Who's that?*

"That's your new name. Fido. From the Latin *fidelis,* meaning 'faithful.' You've got the makings of a faithful dog. A proper *Lincoln* family dog."

We soon came to a wooden house on a corner behind a fence. He opened the front gate and bellowed, "Boys! Come see what I've brought you!"

I peered out between the shawl's folds. Three young 'uns came spilling out the front door. They were like stairsteps, each one taller than the next. The tallest looked like he was waiting for something to come along and impress him. And clearly, I wasn't it. He stayed in the doorway while the other two pelted down the walk.

"What have you got there, Father?" asked the middle-size one.

"A dog, Willie," said Lincoln. "His name is Fido." He set me down gently and pulled aside the shawl.

The boy whooped with joy. "Can I hold him?"

"Gently, Willie, gently. He's had a hard day."

He held me in his arms and stroked me. I

smelled chalk, hickory, rubber. He was a dream of a boy, chock-full of pure joy and mischief.

"Oooh, Taddy!" he said to the littlest one. "Come pet the puppy dog. He has a nice rough coat and a waggly tail."

The littlest one toddled over and stuck his face close to me. I licked it. Maple syrup, smoked hog belly! He sputtered and giggled and called out to his biggest brother, "Bobby, get a doggie kiss!"

But the big boy lingered in the doorway. "I don't care for doggie kisses, Taddy."

"Now, boys, you know Bob is a mite shy of dogs," said Lincoln.

"Bobby got dog bit," said Tad, nodding fiercely.

"And Father had to take him to Terre Haute to get treated by the mad stone," Willie said.

Tad squinted. "Mad th-tone?" His words came out all twisty.

"You remember what a mad stone is, Taddy. It's the hair ball of a deer," Bob said from the doorway. "Supposed to draw out the poison of the dog bite. Mother thinks dogs are dirty and dangerous. She won't like one in the house. Not one bit."

"I guess we'll just have to see. Shall we?" Lincoln lifted me from Willie's arms. He carried me up the front walk and through the door.

Like most tramps, I'd never been inside a house. How'd it feel? Safe, like nothing bad could ever happen inside these walls. It smelled like roasted meat, lemon oil, flowers. Just as I was thinking I'd passed through the gates of Dog Heaven, a shrill scream tore the air.

"TAKE THAT MANGY CUR OUTSIDE!"

She stood at the foot of the stairs. Short and stout, in a big hoop skirt, the missus was as different from her mister as night was from day. He was long and skinny and cool. She was small and round and hotter than blazes. I smelled fire, brimstone, bitter medicine. I burrowed down into the shawl.

"Abraham Lincoln! How *dare* you bring that *creature* into my house! He'll get mud all over."

The two littlest boys clung to their father's coat and began to weep and wail.

"Now, now, Mother," said Lincoln.

She crossed her arms and made her face hard.

In a gentler tone, the man said, "My dear wife, as you can plainly see, the boys have already taken a shine to him."

She scowled, but I could see her face softening.

"Please, my dearest Mary?" Lincoln coaxed.

She sighed. "Well, if you insist on keeping him, take him out to the barn with the others." Then she clutched her head. "I feel a headache coming on. Mr. Lincoln, fetch me a cool cloth."

Lincoln handed me off to Willie. "Outside."

"Don't mind her," Willie whispered to me as he carried me out the back door. "She's excitable."

He set me down near a big old friendly-looking barn. Willie began to toss a ball into the air. I followed it with my eyes. "Chase the ball, Fido!" he said. Then he threw it.

"Chathe it! Chathe it!" Tad lisped.

I stared back at them in puzzlement. Was this ball thing meant for me? I ran and fell on it.

The boys cheered.

Tramps don't know the first thing about balls. I gave it a whiff. It smelled mighty tasty, like the hands of boys who ate with their fingers. I hunkered down in the grass and commenced to eat it.

"Don't *chew* it, Fido. Fetch!" Willie scolded.

I looked up. Willie was giving me such an eager look, I forgot all about the ball. Running at him, I pounced, my paws on his knees. He leaned down, and I licked his face. I knew, then and there, that I would always love this perfect boy.

Willie laughed and and whispered into my fur, "You were supposed to bring the ball with you, silly dog."

We fell over into the grass. Tad piled on. Like three pups, we rolled and tussled. Delicious smells began to beckon from the house. Was this my life from here on in? If so, I was one lucky tramp!

Soon, a ringing bell called an end to our fun. The boys leapt up. Tad toddled off toward the door.

Willie got a rope and gently tied one end around my neck. He tied the other end to a tree. "We'll be back out before you know it, Fido."

My heart sank like a stone. I watched the boys disappear into the house. When I started to follow, the rope tightened around my neck.

Choking, I sank to my haunches. Darkness was falling. That barn didn't look so friendly anymore. I heard scratching inside. Maybe there was a big old bobcat hiding in there. Ma had warned me about them.

Fido, old feller, stand your ground. I sprang to my feet. The fur along my spine stood up. My lips curled into a snarl. I'd show that bobcat that fresh Fido was not the meal for him.

Suddenly, I heard another *scratch.* I yelped and leapt into the air. There followed a squeaking noise, and that's when I saw something wriggle out of a crack in the barn. It waren't no bobcat at all.

It waren't nothing but a dad-blamed, ornery, whippy-tailed gray rat.

2

OLD BOB & CO.

I woke with a start in the dark. The wind had picked up, and my nose twitched. Then I felt Lincoln's big, rough hands gently unfastening the rope from around my neck. I wagged my tail.

You came back!

So had his two sons. They stood behind their pa, shifting from foot to foot, all teary-eyed.

"Now, see here." Lincoln spoke sternly to his

boys. "I don't want to see this dog tied up *ever again.* Is that understood?"

"Yes, Father," said Willie. "We were afraid he would run away."

Tad began to sob. "Taddy love Fido doggie!"

"That's no way to show your love. Better he should run away than strangle himself." He dropped to his knees, eye level with them. "We mustn't ever be cruel to Fido. Nor should he be treated as a prisoner. Now, give him his dinner and bed him down in the barn. He'll be safe there."

"Yes, Father," said Willie. "We're sorry, Fido."

The boys ran off and came back with a big bowl. They set it down before me. It was the kind I'd seen in the laps of womenfolk stringing peas for supper. I poked my nose into it. No peas in this one. It was brimming with delicious meaty scraps!

I wagged my tail and looked up at the boys.

"Go ahead, Fido," said Willie.

"For you, doggie," said Taddy.

This bowl of deliciousness was mine? I dived in and ate it all up. When I had licked away every last drop of goodness, Willie picked me up and carried me into the barn.

Now, hold on just a dad-burned minute, I growled when I saw we were headed for the barn!

Inside, he set down another bowl, this one filled with water. Giving me a quick hug, the boy went away and shut me in!

Didn't they know about the bobcats? I ran to the door and threw myself at it, yelping, *Come back! I don't want to be in here.*

I settled down enough to sniff the measure of the place. Was that horse I smelled? Then I heard a voice from out of the darkness say, *Calm yourself, son. We're all friends here.*

I peered into the gloom and saw a big brown horse in a nearby stall.

Welcome, stranger, he said in a slow horsey way. *The name's Robin, but Lincoln calls me Old Bob. And you are . . . ?*

Fido, I said. *Lincoln says I've got the makings of a faithful dog. A proper Lincoln family dog.*

Well, lardy-dardy for you, said a second voice. A lean tabby cat slid out from the shadows. Behind her I saw the glowing eyes of two or three other cats following her. She sat down and began to lick her paw. The others did the same.

Just so you know, Mr. Fido, said the tabby, *Abe prefers cats to dogs. Ask anyone. The man can't see a cat without stroking it. When he finds a stray cat on the street, he brings it here to the barn to shelter. But I'm the only cat she lets into the house. She hates dogs. HATES them! Says you're dirty and dangerous.*

Go easy on him, Pussums, said Old Bob. *He's just a pup. And besides, I like the name Fido. It means "faithful." A fine quality in a dog.*

This horse sounded for all the world like Lincoln himself. How had this happened? The very next moment, a new voice answered my question.

Don't m-m-mind Old Bob. He's spent so much time carrying Lincoln, the man's wisdom has plumb rubbed off on him. The voice belonged to an old goat. *Billie's the name. Not very original, b-b-but all the same . . .*

I peered around me. *Who else is in here? No bobcats, I hope.*

Old Bob tossed back his head and snickered. *There hasn't been a bobcat in these parts—much less this barn—since my dear old ma was a filly. But there is a milk cow. Daisy, say hello to our new friend.*

Moooooo, said a deep voice near the corncrib.

19

Don't mind her, Old Bob said. *She's a cow of few words. Abe will come to milk her in the morning. Then he'll stake her out in the neighbor's field.*

A man who stoops to milking a cow, spat Pussums. *It's a scandal. Milking is women's work, as everyone knows.* The cats behind her meowed in agreement.

Nay, I say, said Old Bob. *Somebody's got to do it. And Little Missy isn't going to unless Abe's away.*

M-m-milking a cow is far b-b-beneath that one, bleated Billie. *She was brought up for finer things, like sewing and dancing and p-p-poetry.*

Daisy must have found her voice, because she said: *I dooo believe Mr. Lincoln enjoys milking time.*

Old Bob nickered. *Fido, it's a fact that Abe's not afraid of hard work. Why, when Little Missy gets to nagging him, I've seen him come out here and split logs with an ax till he's made a right mountain of kindling. He might be skinny, but he's powerful strong.*

Pussums added silkily, *His hands are rough . . . but tender, especially with us four-leggers.*

He's an animal lover, all right, Old Bob said. *There are folks in this town who'd think nothing of whipping a horse or drowning a cat or stoning a dog—*

Or roasting a b-b-billy goat, said Billie with a shudder.

Yes, it's a well-known fact, said Old Bob. *You won't find a more tenderhearted man anywhere on God's green earth.*

Dog's intuition had already told me that this Lincoln was one fine man. But I was happy to hear my fellow four-leggers sing his praises. If the barn was good enough for them, it was good enough for me. With a snort of relief, I settled down in a pile of straw. I was almost asleep, when I heard Old Bob mutter from his stall.

Mark my words, Fido. Before the week's out, you'll

be inside that house. You've got the makings of a family dog. And a family dog's place is in the house.

Lincoln shoved open the door, and morning sunlight lit up the darkest corners of the barn. He carried a bucket on his arm and a smile on his face. "Good morning, my friends!"

I ran and propped my paws on his knees. *I knew you'd come back!*

He leaned down and scrubbed my fur with his knuckles. "Good morning, Fido!"

He set down a bowl of bread soaked in gravy. I lapped it up while he fed the horse oats, gave the cats milk, and dumped out scraps for the goat.

After I licked my bowl clean, I poked around. Lincoln was leaning into Daisy's side with his long body folded onto a low stool. He was pulling on her udders and squirting liquid into a bucket. I drew closer. Grinning, he shot the spray from one udder into my mouth. I licked my chops. Sweet!

After he finished with the milking, he led Daisy outside to be staked.

When he came back, he held a basket in one hand and a cane in the other. "Follow me, Fido," he said. "We're off to town."

See you folks later! I called out as I dashed to catch up with my man.

Down the street he strode with me at his heels. As he went, he ran the tip of his cane along the pickets of the fences. *Rat-tat-tat-tat.*

When they heard the sound, folks poked their heads out of their windows and called out, "Morning, Mr. Lincoln."

"Morning, Mrs. Shutt! Morning, Mrs. Sprigg! Morning, Mrs. Arnold!" he called back.

Not so very far from the heart of town, we entered a large shed. A man with a long apron stood among pelts of fur and sheets of cured leather. "Good day to you, Bart!" Lincoln said.

"The same to you, Mr. Lincoln. What brings you to the harness shop today?"

"I have need of a collar for Fido here."

The man stroked his chin. He knelt and put a string around my neck. Then he walked over to his bench. Taking a scrap of leather, he snipped and pounded and whistled. In no time, he had fashioned a collar for me. Lincoln fastened it around my neck.

I had seen dogs around town wearing collars. *Make way for me!* they would say with their heads held high. These dogs smelled different—more like people than dogs. Was I now one of them? I was all puffed up with pride as I trotted out of the harness maker's shop.

Lincoln suddenly stopped and looked down at me, stroking his chin thoughtfully. "That's a mighty handsome collar, Fido. But don't you be putting on airs now. Or should I say *hairs*!" He slapped his knee and threw his head back and roared with laughter. "I'll have to remember that one. You don't mind if I make a quick stop at the drugstore, do you, my friend?"

I scampered along behind him.

"Good morning, Mr. Diller," Mr. Lincoln said to the man who met us at the door of the next shop. "I'm here to pick up some powders for Mama and some worm medicine for my dog."

The man peered down at me. I can't say that I cared for the smell of him or his shop. Soap, medicine, poison.

"If you have no objection, Mr. Lincoln, I'll add some spirits of turpentine to your order. Your dog appears to have a case of the mange."

"Thank you kindly, Roland. I'll get the boys to help me dip him this afternoon."

I didn't care for the sound of *that*. But before I could dwell on it, we were out of there.

Just as I was sneezing the drugstore out of my nose, something new tweaked my senses. Meat! I wagged my tail and licked my chops. But when I saw where we were heading, I slowed right down.

Lincoln opened the door of a shop. He turned and looked at me. I sank to my haunches.

I'm fine and dandy, my eyes told him. *How's about I wait for you out here?*

Lincoln cocked a shaggy brow. "I'm not sure I trust a dog that won't set foot in a butcher shop. Come on in, Fido."

I sighed and followed him inside. And me oh my! Everywhere I looked there was meat! Meat hanging from the ceiling. Meat stacked in big glass cases. Meat piled up on the floor. And there, behind the counter, stood the butcher man. He was holding the biggest, juiciest sausage I'd ever seen.

The last time I'd seen this feller in the alley behind his shop was a few days earlier. A couple of us tramps had staked out the back door, begging for scraps. The butcher came out hollering and chased us away with a big, sharp carving knife.

As I watched, he took up the knife. The fur along my spine stood up.

"Your dog looks hungry," said the butcher. He used the knife to cut off the end piece of the sausage. Durned if he didn't toss it right to me! I caught it with a snap of my jaws.

While Lincoln conducted his business, I chewed and wondered: Did the butcher man really not recognize me? Maybe it was the collar. Or the company I was keeping. Or maybe the man had a forgiving soul. Whatever the reason, I was grateful.

I was still licking my chops when Lincoln led me out of the butcher's and into the nearby bakery. It was warm and yeasty-smelling. I licked the crumbs off the floor while Lincoln chatted with the baker man. With a loaf tucked beside the meat, we left there and stopped at the farmer's wagon. Here Lincoln got eggs and vegetables and not much of any interest to me. Basket now full, we headed back home.

I waited on the mat while Lincoln tiptoed in the front door. "Mary!" he called out. There was no answer. After a few moments, he looked at me and shrugged. "I reckon she's still asleep. That means you may safely enter the premises, Fido."

I crept into the front hall and trotted after him into the kitchen. I watched as he unloaded the items from the basket into the larder. Then he paused and listened. I cocked my ear. From somewhere overhead came the sound of boys giggling and horsing around.

"I hear mischief!" Lincoln said, a smile lighting up his craggy face.

I followed him up the steep stairway. We found the younger boys in their father's bedroom. They were standing on his bed a-smacking each other with pillows. The air was filled with feathers. I sneezed. It looked like a henhouse in a fox raid.

"Boys! Boys!" Lincoln whispered loudly, pointing to the next room. "You'll wake Mother."

When they saw me, they squealed and dropped their pillows. I hopped up on the bed, and we celebrated our happy reunion.

Lincoln said, "Time to get dressed, fellers."

He wrestled them out of their bedclothes and

into their daytime duds. Then we all bounded downstairs. We raced past Master Robert, who was sitting at the dining table next to the kitchen.

He looked up from his book. "Mother won't be very happy," he said.

I walked over and sniffed him. Where the boys smelled like Lincoln, this one smelled like brimstone and medicine. Just like his maw.

The boys and I frolicked while Lincoln cooked a mess of eggs and bacon. When it was all served up, I propped my paws on Willie's knees.

"You'll get your chance, Fido," said Willie. He removed my paws and set me back on the floor. I moaned.

"That dog needs some training," Bob said.

"That'll come," Lincoln said.

At the end of the meal, they set their plates down on the floor.

"Have at it, Fido," Lincoln said.

This was more like it. Turned out that Tad was a fussy eater and left me nigh onto a whole plateful of bacon and eggs.

After Lincoln washed the dishes and tidied the kitchen, he took up his tall hat. "All right, fellers! I'm off to the office, and Bob's going to school! Try not to rouse your maw until she's ready. When I get home this evening, I'll worm Fido and dip him in turpentine."

"Can we help?" asked Willie.

"I *expect* nothing less," Lincoln said.

No sooner were Lincoln and Bob gone than Willie's eyes lit up. He rubbed his mitts together. "I've got a grand idea, Taddy! We'll use the water in the washing pan to give Fido a bath. Won't Father be surprised when he comes home?"

The two boys climbed up on a stool. Between

them, they managed to lift the washing pan out and set it on the floor. This was my cue to exit.

"Stay, Fido," said Willie.

I sank to my haunches and watched uneasily while they ran around and fetched bottles and vials. These they opened and dumped into the water. I should have skedaddled when I had the chance. The next thing I knew, Willie grabbed me up and dumped me into the washing pan.

Help! No, no, no, no, no! I whimpered. There were bubbles in my ears and eyes and up my nose! I sneezed and shook myself, soaking the boys. Then bless him if Willie didn't climb right in the tub with me, clothes and all. He took a rough brush and commenced to scrub me. "Isn't this fun, Fido?"

Tad jumped up and down. "Let Taddy in, too!"

"You can't come in," Willie told him. "You'll drown and Father will blame me. Make yourself useful and hand me the turpentine. We'll take care of Fido's mange."

The stuff in that there uncorked bottle smelled powerful bad. Willie dumped it all over me. It stung my skin and burned my nose and eyes. I tried clawing my way out of the tub, but Willie held me tight. Water flooded the kitchen floor. Tad slipped and slid on it, having himself a fine old time.

Just as I was fixing to jump out of my skin, a voice screeched: *"WHAT IN THE NAME OF THE ALMIGHTY IS GOING ON HERE?"*

Little Missy stood in the doorway, her hands on her hips and a deep frown on her face. The boys froze, wide-eyed and guilty as the day is long.

In the sweetest little voice you ever did hear, Willie said, "Good morning, Mother dear. We were just giving Fido a bath so he won't get your fine carpets and furniture all muddy. He smells sweet now on account of we borrowed some of your bath salts from Paris. You don't mind, do you, Mother?"

Her eyes roamed the room. The empty bottles. Her soaking-wet sons. My sopping-wet self. She swelled up like a storm cloud ready to burst. Then, suddenly, all the anger drained out of her. She shook her weary head.

"You wicked, *wicked* little imps! You *would* make a mess like this on the maid's day off. It'll take me the rest of the day to clean it up."

"We're sorry, Mother," said Willie. "We'll help."

"Some help *you'll* be," she said with a snort. "Oh, wipe the pitiful looks off your faces. I give up. You may keep your dog in the house. Far be it from me to come between you and your tramp. Just remember," she added sternly, "no muddy paws."

And that is how, even sooner than old Bob had foretold, I came to be the Lincoln Family Dog.

GONE FISHIN'

What with all them tasty vittles, I was fully growed in no time. At two years of age, I was also smart enough to know what was what.

"That dog is bright as a penny," Lincoln said.

But Little Missy hadn't changed her mind about me one iota. Far as she was concerned, I was still dirty and dangerous.

I was dirty because I tracked in mud. She'd screech when she saw my paw prints and go running for her washrags. She had Aunt Mariah, the maid, to help her clean. But I think she liked doing it herself. Little Missy was the cleaningest lady I ever did see, always dropping to her knees, scrubbing and scowling. But it waren't my fault. The streets of Springfield were a right pigsty.

I was dangerous, too, the way she saw it. My way of saying howdy was to jump up on the boys and prop my big paws on their chests. When I was a pup, it was cute and harmless. But now I was big enough to bowl them clean over. Not that the boys cared. They just laughed and picked themselves up.

"One day you'll crack your silly skulls and then you'll be laughing out of the other side of your faces," she told them. "You'd best cure your dog of that bad habit or else."

They never did cure me. I think they liked me the way I was.

But my ways waren't *all* bad.

I was good about answering nature's calls. I scratched at the back door until someone let me out. Having done my duty, I scratched to get in. Little Missy was not happy with the scratch marks on her door. Still, I believe she preferred them to dog doo on the divan.

I was good about keeping off the furniture. There was only one piece in the house I was allowed on. It was a great long couch covered in horsehair cloth. I slept on it and napped on it. When I was afeared, I hid beneath it. Lincoln had had it made to fit his great long body.

"Ugly old piece of furniture isn't fit for anything *but* a dog," Little Missy said.

Mostly, I had the couch to myself because Lincoln was away. He was *traveling the circuit*. Being a dog, I did not rightly know the meaning of this. But Old Bob set me straight.

It has to do with lawyering, Old Bob said.

What's lawyering? I asked.

It's the job Lincoln does. He stands up for people's rights.

Hmmm, I said. *I stand up on my hind legs when I say howdy. Is that the same thing?*

Not exactly, the horse said. *It's more like what he did when he first met you. He stood up for you against those nasty boys. On the circuit, he stands up for folks when someone damages their property or steals their livestock or is accused of wrongdoing.*

How'd you get to be so learned on the subject? I asked.

Once, I was the one who carried him from town to town on the circuit. But now the railroad does it.

While Lincoln was away on the circuit, Little Missy took on the marketing, the cooking, the washing, and sometimes even the milking. She had energy and grit. But come nighttime, she turned into a shivering pile of petticoats. She was afeared some good-for-nuthin' thief would steal into the house and rob her blind. She ordered me to stand at the foot of her bed and guard her all the night.

"Earn your keep, dog," she told me, "and be a proper watchdog."

One night a storm blew up. A bolt of lightning hit the tree outside the window. Next moment, thunder rumbled so loud, it shook the house.

RUN FOR COVER! I howled as I dived under Little Missy's wardrobe. All night long, that storm raged. When it blew over in the early hours, I figured it was safe to come out. But I'd wedged myself in there so deep I was well and truly stuck! That's where she found me come morning.

Little Missy screeched for the boys, who came

running. Did they ever laugh at the sight of me!

"Stuck," said Willie, "like a pig between the pickets. What do you think, Tad? Do we grease him up to pull him out?"

I gazed out from under the wardrobe with sad eyes. *Have pity!*

"Silly old dog," he said.

He and Tad each grabbed a leg and tugged me

loose. I didn't even stop to say thank you. I slinked away to my couch, my dog dignity badly bent. Some watchdog I'd turned out to be!

But I didn't feel bad for long. After all, I had me a gang to call my own. A whole slew of us ran together in a pack. There was Isaac, the druggist's son, and little Johnny Kaine. There were the three DuBois boys—Fred, Jess, and Link—and Josie Remann and her brother, Henry. All five of Dr. and Mrs. Melvin's boys. And then there were the Rolls—Johnny and Frankie. The Roll boys being younger than the rest, I'd follow them home evenings and make sure they got there safe.

The gang's usual game was Town Ball. They played it with a rubber ball and a slat borrowed from a picket fence. Every so often, I'd grab the ball myself. That set off a brand-new game they called Get the Ball Back from Fido.

Other times, they played Blindman's Bluff. With all those young 'uns stumbling about, I had to look lively or I'd be trampled underfoot.

But the most dangerous game was Mumblety-Peg. Each player took a turn throwing a jackknife into the dirt and then lunging after it in a single step. In those days, mothers let their sons play with sharp knives. When I heard the word *Mumblety-Peg,* I'd take cover in the nearest bush!

My personal favorite was Circus. It was the kids' own version of the circus that now and then came to town. The gang would post signs all over, string bunting along the fence, and charge buttons for admission. In our backyard, Willie swung from a tree branch like a trapeze artist. Link was a magician, pulling rabbits and pigeons from his pa's tall hat. Daring Josie sailed high on a wooden swing. But the star of the circus was a certain yaller dog.

In exchange for treats, I would sit, roll over, and fetch.

Whenever Lincoln was home, he joined in the fun. Many was the afternoon he would take off from lawyering to shoot a game of marbles or spin a top or fly a kite with the boys.

One summer's day, he came home early from lawyering and said to Tad and Willie, "We're goin' fishin', boys. Let's hitch up Old Bob."

We came barging into the barn carrying fishing poles and a hamper of goodies. You should have seen the look on Old Bob's face.

Oh, happy day! the horse whickered. Lincoln picked the rocks from his hooves while the boys soaped up his bridle and harness. *It's one thing to take Little Missy to visit friends. But stepping out with Abe holding the reins is a rare privilege. It brings back the good old days of riding the circuit—and that's a fact.*

With Bob hitched up, we all clambered aboard the buggy. The old horse proudly pulled us through town toward the Sangamon River. As we passed by, the other children poured out of their houses.

"Grab your fishing poles and climb aboard!" Lincoln called out to them.

The youngest Melvin boy blubbered, "I don't got no fishing pole."

"Don't worry, little man!" Lincoln called back. "We'll rig you up something good."

Mrs. Melvin came out, shaking her head. "Abraham Lincoln, you're a veritable Pied Piper."

"Don't you worry, Mrs. Melvin. I'll have your boys back before supper."

All afternoon, we dug for worms and fished for fish and feasted on the banks of the Sangamon. As the sun began to sink, we loaded up and Old Bob took us back to town. He stopped to let off each tired and muddy young 'un at their front door.

When we got to our door, Little Missy was there waiting for us. She was tapping her foot and looking fit to be tied. "Just where have you been? I hope you don't expect *me* to cook dinner."

"No worries. We've brought our dinner with us, Mother." Lincoln held up a bucket of river trout.

Little Missy made a face like she'd just eaten a

rotten pawpaw. "You'll have to clean them yourselves. I can't stand the feel of fish guts."

"Don't worry, Mother," said Willie sweetly.
"Taddy and Fido and me *love* fish guts."

But all was not fun and fish guts. One day, I followed Lincoln a ways out of town to the boneyard,
otherwise known as Hutchinson Cemetery. There,
Lincoln made his way in and out of the rows
until we came to the small stone marker in the
corner.

Lincoln took off his tall hat and held it over his
heart. He stared down at the stone and spoke:

"Edward B.

Son of A. & M. Lincoln

DIED Feb. 1, 1850.

Age 3 years 10 months 18 days

Of such is the kingdom of Heaven."

After we had visited a few times, I understood. Lincoln had three sons in the house on the corner. And a fourth lying in the earth under that small stone.

"Eddy wasn't four years old when he went," he said to me. "Once, when Mary and the two boys were visiting family in Lexington, Eddy adopted a stray kitten. How that child loved cats! Mary's stepmother hated them and kicked the poor thing out of the house. Eddy screamed and yelled and carried on. I always say you can tell a lot about a person from the way he treats animals. He was a fine little boy and would have grown into a fine man."

Just like his father. Of that I had no doubt.

4

A HOUSE DIVIDED

Every Sunday, Little Missy dressed to the nines and went to church. Sometimes, she took the boys with her. Other times, she left them with Lincoln. Often as not, he would take them to his lawyering office in town. He'd get them settled in with some marbles. Then he'd go and bury his head in the pile of papers. He didn't pay those lads the slightest mind. So what happened next? A mountain of mischief!

Willie's noggin was chock-full of mischief.

And Tad had begun to make a fair study of it, too. They'd run around and build a tall mountain out of papers and books and anything else they could find that wasn't nailed down. Then they'd sprinkle the top with ashes from the wood stove. Howling with wild glee, the two would climb up the mountain and stomp them ashes into the paper and books.

Hey, Lincoln! I'd bark. *Pay some mind to what's going on right under your nose!*

But did he listen to me? Not one little bit. So I lay down, nose on paws, and fretted. Meanwhile, Lincoln's partner, Mr. Herndon, sat at his desk and wagged his head in pure dismay.

"Little devils," he muttered. He looked like he wanted to wring their necks. But he held back.

Still, even young Herndon had his limits—and he met them on a Sunday after the young 'uns had gotten into a shelf of lawyer books. As evening fell,

Lincoln got up and shook himself off like a dog coming in out of the rain. He called the boys to him and took their hands and led them toward the door, stepping over the unholy mess they'd made. Either he didn't notice it or he didn't care. His mind was somewhere else. That's the kind of feller he was. Head in the clouds.

Mr. Herndon finally spoke up. "If they were mine, I'd take off my shoe and give them a licking they'd never forget."

Lincoln's eyes flashed. "It is my pleasure that my children are free, happy, and unrestrained by parental tyranny. Love is the chain whereby to bind a child to his parents."

That was Lincoln for you. One deep thinker.

Mr. Herndon wasn't the only person in town who took a dim view of Lincoln's methods of raising up his young. One day—I must have been three years old and then some—I followed Lincoln over to Judge Treat's office.

The two men sat playing chess and jawing about politics. Don't ask me what politics is. It was a topic that got everyone in town all fired up. Everyone but me. They yammered. I slept. Suddenly, I woke as Tad came bursting through the door.

He was a young lad now, of maybe five years, but he was still as tongue-twisted as ever. He stood there, struggling. I knew how he felt. We dogs often suffer when we try to express ourselves. Lacking human voice, we fail often as not. But Lincoln never had any trouble understanding Tad. That day, he was telling Lincoln to come home for supper.

Lincoln waved Tad off. "Run along and tell Mother I'll be home by and by, Taddy."

Tad went away. Some time later, he came marching back. The men were still at their game.

Again, Tad asked and Lincoln said, "Soon, Taddy. Run along." The third time rolled around. Lincoln was still at the game. In a fit of botheration, the lad brought his knee up beneath the table and jolted the board. Game pieces went flying.

"Home NOW!" He stomped his foot.

Judge Treat was madder than a wet hen.

"You ought to punish the boy," he said to Lincoln. "He has ruined our game!"

Lincoln smiled slyly. "Considering the position of your pieces, Judge, at the time of the upheaval, I think you had no reason to complain."

Lincoln, an easy father and a wily lawyer, was about to become famous for his speechifying.

In June of 1858, a big meeting called the State Convention had come to town. Men flocked from all over to meet and gab. When they were finished with their meeting and gabbing, they announced that Lincoln was their choice for something called the United States Senate.

Lincoln told us that night at the dinner table: "It appears I am running for office."

Little Missy was thrilled to her toes. So were the boys. But I was puzzled. *Running?* Lincoln, *running?* Striding, always. Loping, sometimes. But I don't believe I'd ever seen the man *run*. And not ever to the office.

As usual, I looked to Old Bob for answers. He told me the office in question was not Lincoln's lawyering one but a government office. He said Lincoln was running a race *against* another man to win that office, a slick feller named Stephen Douglas. People called him the Little Giant. He was a little man with stubby legs. I figured Lincoln, with his long ones, would lick him.

The Little Giant and Lincoln didn't see eye to eye. They took turns speechifying before crowds to see how many people they could win over to their side. That's how they'd get votes and win this race.

When I followed him to his lawyering office

one day, Lincoln invited me in and then locked the door. He said to his partner, "Will you listen to my speech? I think Fido's had his fill of it."

I'd heard him speechifying under his breath for days now.

"If it's the speech you're giving tomorrow at the hall of the House of Representatives, I'd love to hear it," said Mr. Herndon.

I settled down to gnaw on a bit of cowhide

I had stashed beneath the desk. Lincoln paced. In his high, twangy voice, he commenced:

"Mr. President and gentlemen of the convention. If we could first know *where* we are, and *whither* we are tending, we could then better judge *what* to do, and *how* to do it.

"We are now far into the *fifth* year, since a policy was initiated, with the *avowed* object, and *confident* promise, of putting an end to slavery agitation.

"Under the operation of that policy, that agitation has not only *not ceased*, but has *constantly augmented*. In *my* opinion, it *will* not cease, until a *crisis* shall have been reached, and passed. A house divided against itself cannot stand. I believe this government cannot endure, permanently half *slave* and half *free*. I do not expect the Union to be *dissolved*—I do not expect the house to *fall*—but I *do* expect it will cease to be divided. It will become *all* one thing or *all* the other. Either the *opponents* of slavery, will arrest the further spread of it, and place it where the public mind shall rest in the belief that it is in the course of ultimate extinction; or its *advocates* will push it forward, till it shall become alike lawful in *all* the States, *old* as well as *new*—*North* as well as *South*. . . ."

A dog's age later, Lincoln finished. Mr. Herndon rubbed his face and sighed. "I don't know, Mr. Lincoln. . . . It may not be politic. Are people ready to hear it?"

Lincoln unlocked the door and went outside. Soon, he came back trailing a passel of men. They listened as he gave the speech again.

When he was finished, no one said a word for the longest time.

Then one man leaned back in his chair and

frowned. "Abe, you can't say that! It will stir up a hornet's nest."

A second man said, "It's a good speech, but it is too far ahead of its time."

"I, for one," put in a third, "would like to hear the words finally said."

The men fell to arguing in loud voices. Finally, Herndon's voice rose above the din.

"Lincoln, deliver it as it reads. If it is in advance of the times, let us lift the people to its level. The speech is true, wise, and politic, and will succeed now or in the future. Nay. It will aid you, if it will not make you president of the United States."

President of the United States. The words were new to my ears. But in time, they would become all too familiar. And that was just too durned bad for me, as you'll see for yourself, by and by.

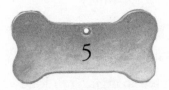

BILLY THE BARBER

Lincoln and Douglas did their speechifying all over the state. The Lincoln-Douglas debates, folks called them. I was nearly four years old, and I thought I had seen and heard everything. But when those two spoke in Springfield, you would have thought the circus had come to town. Banners flew and bands played and people marched in the streets.

All this fuss and ruckus came as an unwelcome surprise to me. In case you haven't already figured it out, I like to enjoy my peace and quiet.

I was sleeping under a bush in the front yard, when I heard the terrible noise for the first time. It was a *pop! pop! popping!* so sudden and so loud that it came pretty close to *stop-stop-stopping* my heart. What in the world was it? I knew—and dreaded—the sound of gunfire. Had somebody come a-gunning for me?

When Willie came upon me whimpering in the bush, he knelt down and stroked me, grinning ear to ear. "It's all right, boy. Them's just firecrackers. Folks are celebrating Father. He's a regular home-town hero. They're happy."

If this is what people did when they were happy, well then, I wished them a whole lot less happiness.

Election Day came. It was cold and rainy, not fit for a dog. Still, all of Springfield turned out to vote. Lincoln was their man.

But folks in other towns voted for the Little Giant. Lincoln lost the race. Stephen Douglas got the government office in the Senate, and Lincoln returned to lawyering. While defeat didn't seem to bother Lincoln any, his sons were dashed. They had had such high hopes the old man would win.

But wouldn't you know there was a new election coming down the pike? And this one was even bigger than the last. The town was buzzing with talk of Lincoln running for president. I still did not know a president from a tobacco plug. But his little boys perked right up. I heard their excited whispers as they lay in their bed at night. I think they sensed that their pa would win this election and their lives would change forever.

The idea of change didn't do nothing but worry me. If there's anything we dogs hate, it's change.

And things *were* changing, whether I liked it

or not. I knew this because it was me who carried the mail home from the post office every day, holding the letters in my mouth. Unlike watchdogging, this was one chore I did well. But beginning one day—what was this?—there were too many letters to fit in my mouth!

On the outside, Lincoln hadn't changed. He still wore the same hat and the same swallowtail coat. He still wore the same high-water pants and dusty boots. But inside the man, a fire burned. It lit up his pale eyes and the spirits of everyone around him. Now, as he strode down the streets of Springfield, people would tip their hats and look at him in a new way.

They noticed it at the barbershop, too. Three times a week, rain or shine, we went down to the shop with the shiny striped pole next to the front door. Inside, Lincoln would sit down in a big chair and get his hair cut and the fur shaved off his face.

The barber was named Mr. William Florville. He was a man from a faraway island. Folks in town called him Billy the Barber. Every so often, he liked to strike up a tune on his fiddle. Lincoln would lounge around the shop with the other men. His long legs stretched out before him, he swapped stories and shared news. But nowadays he held forth on politics as well.

Outside the shop, we dogs lay on the walkway, waiting for our humans to reappear. It was a chance to swap stories and share news, too. And, yes, hold forth on politics in our own way.

Carlo, a white bulldog, was our leader. He was Billy the Barber's dog. A little black poodle, name of Jenny Lind, was also a regular. She was the cunning little canine companion of a newspaperman. All three of us were decked out in collars made by

Bart, the harness maker. We knew that these collars
set us apart from the others. Not that I'm putting
on "hairs" as Lincoln would say. But the fact is, we
knew more about what was going on in the world
than your typical Springfield tramp.

Carlo lifted his big head. *Fido, my friend, they*

say your man is headed for the White House.

I sure hope not, I said with a shiver. *I like the house we're in now.*

He's hungry for it. Billy says so. And I daresay that no human in this town knows Lincoln better than my Billy, with the exception of his law partner. Just the other day, Herndon came in for a shave. He was saying that Lincoln's going to be the next president.

Let's hope he's wrong. I heaved a sigh.

How can you be so selfish? Jenny poked her pretty little nose in my face. *This country needs him! Slavery is dividing the nation.*

What's this slavery business everybody keeps jawing about? I said.

It's about black and white, said Carlo.

How do you mean? I asked.

You can see with your own eyes that Lincoln and most of the people in this town are white. You can also see that Billy—like Reverend Brown and Mr. Jenkins on your street—is black, said Carlo.

To tell you the dog's honest truth, I never gave it much thought. Aunt Mariah, who cooks and does the laundry for us, is black, too. But all people are alike to me, black and white. All dogs are, too. You're white and Jenny is black—but you're both the same to me.

Carlo and Jenny shared a look.

Would that more people felt the way you do, dear Fido, said Jenny. *This country wouldn't be in such deep trouble. But some whites think that blacks are ignorant and inferior and should live in chains.*

From inside the shop, Billy struck up his fiddle. Usually, he played a lively jig. But today, the tune was sad. It brought to mind the way I'd felt trussed up in the feed sack. Was this what it felt like to be a slave? Helpless and afeared and unloved?

Lucky for me, Lincoln felt about dogs the same

way he did about people. He thought we all de-
served kindness and respect. Billy's sad fiddling
worked its way deep into my heart. Before I knew
it, I had opened my mouth and begun to howl.

Why, Fido! Jenny Lind said. *Who knew you had
such a lovely singing voice!*

My tail thumped against the sidewalk. Could
it be that the lovely Miss Jenny Lind had taken a
shine to homely old me?

6

VOTE FOR OLD ABE!

Folks in Springfield loved their parties. They were the getting-togetherest people you ever did see. They got together for weddings, new babies, birthdays, graduations, funerals, holidays, strawberry-picking, you name it. Sometimes, the parties were for the young whippersnappers. Other times, they were for the grown-ups. Whole families went out for squeezes. They were parties thrown for no reason at all but to say howdy-do.

But tonight's party wasn't a squeeze. It was a hoity-toity shindig for grown-ups, the kind of party Little Missy loved. It gave her a chance to doll up and douse herself with Paris perfume.

Like all dogs, I don't care for perfume. It got up inside my nose. I couldn't smell anything but that dad-blamed perfume. A dog *sees* the world with his nose. A dog with a fuddled sense of smell? Why, he's no better than a cat that can't mouse.

The boys had just come home from a party of their own: a candy pull. At candy pulls, young 'uns stood around a table. On the table was a large blob of boiled molasses called taffy.

Taffy! Just the word made me drool. The children would reach into the mess. They'd pull the taffy into long strings of sweet, chewy candy and lower it into their open mouths, like baby birds eating worms. Ate themselves sick often as not.

Lincoln was fixing to bathe his sticky young 'uns and tuck them into their bed. But the little boys wouldn't hear of it.

"We want to go to the party, too!" they whined.

You may have noticed that when whipper-snappers get too many sweets, they kick up a fuss.

Little Missy smoothed her silky skirts and glared at them. "We're going to the Duboises' house. It's a party for *grown-ups*. You stay home with Robert."

"We don't want to stay home with Robert!" they howled. "We want to go with you!"

"This will never do," said Lincoln. "Mother, if you'll let the boys go, I will take care of them."

Little Missy growled. "Why, Father! You know it's no place for boys to be."

"I'll bring them in the back door and leave them in the kitchen," Lincoln said.

With a stomp of her little foot, she said, "Oh,

very well. Have it your way. You always do!"

Lincoln washed the sticky off the lads and dressed them in their Sunday best. Then we all set out for the shindig. The party house was lit up like a riverboat and chock-full of folks dressed in fancy duds gabbing away at the top of their voices. It was enough to make me turn around and run home to my couch. But I knew my duty.

I kept an eye on the boys. The noise of the party had put me off my feed. But the boys were hungrier than calves in a corncrib. In their greedy little mitts, they grabbed the food off the trays and began to stuff themselves. Willie's mouth being bigger, he ate more. Not to be outdone by his brother, Tad grabbed himself a whole roasted ham by the string.

"Yahoo!" He galloped off. Willie and I scrambled after, him yelling, me barking.

The guests gasped and parted to make way
for us. Like a Wild West cowboy with a lasso, Tad
swung the ham by the string. Little Missy nearly
popped her stays! But Lincoln just laughed.

"Come, Taddy." He swept up boy and ham beneath his arm and disappeared into the kitchen. A silence fell over the party. They were waiting to hear the crack of Lincoln's hand on Tad's behind. But no such sound came. Not then. Not ever.

No matter how naughty his boys got, Lincoln was the kindest, gentlest father that ever did live.

Later that same month, my world was blown clean off its hinges. I went with Lincoln to the offices of the *Daily Illinois State Journal.* Truth to tell, I was hoping to run into Miss Jenny Lind. We had grown kind of sweet on each other. I was hoping to do a little courting and sparking.

But the moment we walked into the room, all thoughts of courtship were plumb wiped away. Half of Springfield had crowded into that stuffy little office. Men greeted Lincoln in loud voices:

"If it isn't Old Abe!"

"The Rail-Splitter himself!"

"Are you prepared to accept the nomination, Honest Abe?"

The crowd swallowed him up. Just as I was fixing to run home, Jenny came sashaying up to me.

Hello, Fido, she said. *I've been waiting for you.*

She led me beneath a table, where the two of us settled down cheek by jowl.

Isn't this exciting? she asked.

I grunted. *If you like loud noise.* My idea of excitement was playing Town Ball with the gang. This—men laughing and booming and smoking cigars—was not for me.

You'd better get used to it, she said. *The Republican National Convention is happening right now in Chicago. They're about to choose who will run for the office of president of the United States.*

Not that president business again! Don't tell me,
I moaned, *they're going to choose Lincoln.*

She nodded. *Any minute now, that telegraph key
over there is going to start clicking and clacking. And
when it does, this entire room is going to explode.*

I leapt to my feet. *Explode? You mean, blow up?
Like a big old firecracker?*

She laughed. *Sit down, silly boy. I mean explode
with excitement.*

That was plenty bad as far as I was concerned. I headed for the door. *Thanks for the warning!*

Fido! Where are you going? she called after me.

Not even for this pretty little lady was I going to stick around. *Home,* I called back to her, *where it's safe!*

I scratched at the door, and some kindly gent let me out. As I trotted down the stairs, I heard him say, "Who owns the yaller dog?"

"Don't you know?" someone else said. "That's the Lincoln Dog. Soon, he'll be as famous as his master."

MISCHIEF ARTISTS

That night, it became official. Lincoln was nominated to run for president of the United States. An artist named Thomas Hicks came in June to paint the candidate's picture. Little Missy was busy shopping, so the boys and I went with him. Lincoln sat posing at his desk, holding a pen over a sheet of paper. He had his head in the clouds. The artist, his beady eyes moving from Lincoln to the easel, dabbed away with a paintbrush.

As usual, Lincoln had no idea what his boys were up to. But Mr. Hicks saw all too well. The little fellers had gotten into his box of paints. They grabbed the fat tubes, unscrewed the caps, and began to squirt out great globs of paint.

In no time, paint covered their hands and arms. The imps smeared their fingers on the walls and made big messy swirls. Soon, their faces and hair and clothing were as paint-smeared as the walls.

Finally, Lincoln came down from the clouds. "Boys! Boys!" he said. "You mustn't meddle with Mr. Hicks's paints. Now run home and have your faces and hands washed."

Lincoln may have been ready to rule the republic. But his little sons still ruled his heart.

In the portrait by Hicks, you'll note that Lincoln had no fur on his face. His face was still shaved clean. This was yet one more thing that was about

to change. Some months after sitting for Hicks,
Lincoln got a letter from a little girl. The day I
carried it home from the post office, he slit it open
and read it aloud.

"Listen to this, boys. This letter is from Grace Bedell of Westfield, New York. It seems she's worried about my looks. 'If you let your whiskers grow . . . you would look a great deal better, for your face is so thin. All the ladies like whiskers and they would tease their husbands to vote for you and then you would be president.'

"What do you say, boys? Should I grow a beard?" Lincoln asked, his eyes dancing with mischief.

Willie stroked his chin as if he himself had whiskers. "It might make you look wiser."

But Tad made a face. "Too scratchy," he said.

Lincoln had always longed for a daughter. It was a disappointment to him that he and Mary had only had boys. Maybe that's how he came to heed Grace Bedell's advice. One day in early November, he and I went down to the barbershop.

"Billy," he told his friend, "let's give my whiskers a chance to grow."

From that day on, Lincoln sported a face full of fur. They held the flavor of the food he ate. This was *one* change I liked.

Just before Election Day that same year, people lined up outside the house to shake Lincoln's hand. The new scents they brought with them fuddled and vexed me. Lincoln had his own problems. The man shook so many hands that his shaking hand swelled and cracked like a dried-up gourd.

Strangers came inside without even knocking. They walked through our rooms like they owned the place. They tried to coax me out from beneath the couch and called to each other, "Come pet the Lincoln Dog!"

For the love of dog, couldn't they just leave the Lincoln Dog in peace?

One day, I was sitting with Willie and Tad on the front step. Suddenly, a group of strange gents came through the gate and up the walk. They smelled of meat, liquor, tobacco.

Willie whispered to his brother, "I think these are the men from Washington who nominated Pa."

"Are you Mr. Lincoln's son?" one of them asked Willie.

"Yes, sir," said the eager nine-year-old.

"Then let's shake hands." The man thrust out his big hand and Willie shook it.

Then Tad piped up. "I'm a Lincoln, too!"

After Tad got his shaking, the man turned to me. "And this must be the famous Lincoln Dog." He reached out a hand.

Did he expect me to shake his hand, too? That was one slick trick the boys had never taught me. And even if they had, I would not have done it for him, smelling the way he did. I did not want to entertain these strangers. I wanted them off my property and out of my life. I growled. But they walked right past me and into the house.

I followed them in and glared as they made themselves at home on *my* horsehair couch. Why, those low-down varmints! I growled a little louder in case they hadn't heard me.

Little Missy swept in. "Mr. Lincoln will be back soon. We weren't expecting you this early."

"Your dog seems upset," one of the men said. "Is it something we've done?"

"Of course not," she said, then turned to me. "You can share your couch for one day." She said to the gents, "Don't mind Fido. He thinks he's a fierce watchdog, but he's really a bit of a coward."

Ouch.

8

ONE HUNDRED GUNS

I came awake with a start late on the day of the election. Lincoln, who had been out watching the voting, banged open the front door. He strode to the foot of the stairs. He called up, "Mother! We won!"

Little Missy rushed downstairs.

"Well, hello, Mr. President," she cooed.

He caught her up in his arms and swung her around. Willie and Tad joined them and hung on his coattails. I was just about to jump in, when I heard a thundering *BOOM!*

Cannon fire! We were under attack!

Back beneath the couch I dived.

My family burst out laughing. That cut me to the quick.

"Fido, you'd better get used to the noise," Lincoln said. "Come out and join us."

But I wouldn't. It waren't safe. I heard cheers, drums, music, all growing louder as it moved closer to the house. I shrank back into the shadows, trying to make myself as small as possible.

"It seems our friends and neighbors are in a mood to celebrate," chirped Little Missy.

The family went outside.

Then someone started shooting guns.

BANG! BANG! BANG! BANG!

The noise was so loud I thought my brain

would explode. I'm no stranger to gunfire. But Willie or Tad usually came to comfort me. Now they had abandoned me.

After the election, the house was in an uproar. Little Missy was busy with her maid, stitching up gowns fit for a president's mate. Newspapermen from out of town came to talk to Lincoln. Friends and neighbors walked through the house, poking around and looking over the furniture.

"We're selling it all," Little Missy told them. "We're getting all new furniture for the White House."

Lincoln cleared his throat. "We're not selling *all* of it, Mother," he said.

She flicked a sour glance at me. "Of course not, Father," she said sweetly. "Not that hideous couch of yours. It's not fit for anyone but a dog."

Lincoln smiled. "That's exactly who it *is* fit for, Mary. And why we dare not sell it."

The boys bragged to the gang about their pa's new job. Bob came home from school back east. I barely recognized him in his fancy suit and stiff collar. He smelled different, too—of faraway places.

There was so much going on in the house that my head spun. Every time I looked, another piece of furniture was missing. No more cozy rooms. Only empty rooms that echoed loudly.

And then came that dreadful day. While I was out and about, someone had come and swiped my horsehair couch!

When I got home, I ran around the parlor barking. *Where is it? Who took our couch?*

I jumped up on Lincoln. *Find the low-down dirty varmint who made off with our couch!*

"Calm down, now, Fido." Lincoln knelt down

and gave me a hug. Then he pulled away and said
in a choked-up voice, "You best go with the boys.
They'll show you where your couch is. Boys?"

The boys huddled in the doorway. When I
saw they were sniffling and tearful, I ran over and

jumped up on them. I licked their salty faces. *Don't cry! Who needs a couch when I have you!*

Willie looked to his father, his eyes streaming. "Father! Please, please, don't make us do this," he begged. "Fido is part of the family. He needs to come with us to Washington."

"Please, please, please, Papa?" Tad begged. He wiped his runny nose on his sleeve.

Lincoln shook his head sorrowfully. "How are we to get him there? Trains are a noisy means of transportation. Every town we pass through will likely fire off its cannon. And even if, by however miracle, we could get him to Washington, he'd hate it," he said. "You saw how he reacted to the election celebrations, cowering under the couch, howling at the ruckus. In Washington, there will be no end of ruckus. The bells of a dozen churches will ring countless times every day. There'll be cannons and gunfire and brass bands and mobs larger—and angrier—than any we've seen in Springfield. Think of how miserable the poor creature will be.

"We mustn't be selfish, boys. Fido is a simple dog. He belongs in Springfield, living a simple life. We'll be moving into the Chenery House for our last few days in town before we leave. Dogs aren't allowed. You boys show Fido to his new home."

I didn't understand what was happening. But I knew my boys were sad and I had to fix that. I ran ahead of them down the front walk and wagged my tail, cheering them on. That's when I happened to see Old Bob being led away down the street. *Where are you going?* I said.

To Flynn's barn. Lincoln is leaving Springfield, and he can't take me with him. What about you?

I don't know, I said. *I don't know anything anymore.*

I hurried to rejoin the boys. I was happy when they turned in at the Roll house. I followed them up the familiar walkway and through the open front door. It was like they'd been expecting us.

And there, in a corner of their parlor, was my horsehair couch!

My heart leapt. I ran and jumped onto it. I rolled on my back with such joy you'd have thought it was a field of sweet clover.

The Roll boys, Johnny and Frankie, climbed up onto the couch with me.

"Hello, boy!" Johnny said.

"You're gonna be living with us from now on," said Frankie.

The boys wrapped their arms around me, and I licked their faces.

The next time I looked up, Willie and Tad were gone.

FAREWELL

In the next few days, I stayed at the Rolls' house and seldom left the horsehair couch. This was Lincoln's couch, too. I figured that anytime now he'd walk in the door and lie down next to me. And where Lincoln went, the boys weren't far behind.

I'd get up now and then. I'd lost my appetite, but that didn't mean Mother Nature stopped calling. When she did, I'd slip off the couch and scratch at the back door.

"Boys, go out with him," Mr. Roll said the first time I did this. "I promised I wouldn't tie him up. I also promised we'd keep a sharp eye on him."

"Yes, Pa," said Johnny and Frankie.

Once we were outside, Johnny said to his brother, "Is Fido more important to Pa than we are? We ain't allowed to track mud into the house, but Fido is. How come that is?"

"I reckon it's cause Pa made a promise to Mr. Lincoln. Fido can track in mud and run around free and come and go as he pleases. Pa aims to keep his promise. He says it ain't every day you get to keep a promise to the president of the United States."

They waited as I answered nature's call. Then I cut and ran down the street to the old house on the corner. The boys tore after me.

I went to the back door and scratched to get

in. I scratched and scratched until the claw marks were even deeper. But no one came to the door. I did this day after day, every time I went out.

"Ain't nobody home, Fido," Johnny said to me.

I ran around and jumped up to look in the windows. The house stood silent and empty. Weary and defeated, I returned to the Rolls' house.

A few days later, on a rainy day in February, I followed them a ways east. Soon, I heard a loud, rushing noise up ahead. It sounded like a roaring river overflowing its banks. But I knew it was no river. It was an excited crowd.

Then I saw the people, filling the open area around the railroad tracks. They were gathered before the depot of the Great Western Railroad. A giant steam engine stood on the tracks, its pipes smoking and hissing.

The people were standing in the rain, their

dripping umbrellas overlapping. There were women and men, black and white, children and parents and old folks. There were reporters, too, licking their pencil tips, with their pads in hand. Something mighty important was about to happen.

Suddenly, the crowd burst into cheers. I flinched at the noise. But what was this? Lincoln strode out onto the platform on those long legs with his long arms dangling from his too-short sleeves. He hadn't left town, after all!

I leapt up and barked.

"Stay," said Johnny, gripping my collar.

I wanted to go to Lincoln. He looked so lonely up there. But the boys held on tight to me and I stayed put. I watched as Lincoln's wintry eyes roved the faces gathered before him.

"My friends," he began in a voice that shook, "no one, not in my situation, can appreciate my

feeling of sadness at this parting. To this place,
and the kindness of these people, I owe everything. Here I have lived a quarter of a century, and
have passed from a young to an old man. Here

my children have been born, and one is buried. I now leave, not knowing when, or whether ever, I may return, with a task before me greater than that which rested upon Washington. Without the assistance of that Divine Being, who ever attended him, I cannot succeed. With that assistance I cannot fail. Trusting in Him, who can go with me, and remain with you and be everywhere for good, let us confidently hope that all will yet be well. To His care commending you, as I hope in your prayers you will commend me, I bid you an affectionate farewell."

Folks wept. They raised their hands, waving their hats and hankies. With a final lift of his hand, Lincoln climbed onto the train. With sad eyes, I watched the train carry him away.

This time, I knew he was really gone.

❈   ❈   ❈

Old habits die hard, and I kept returning to the house on the corner. But strangers soon moved in and they ran me off. My place now was in my new home with my new boys.

I'll say this for them: the Rolls treated me royally. Mr. Roll saved the best table scraps for me. Mrs. Roll never once scolded me for tracking in mud. Johnny and Frankie became almost as dear to me as Willie and Tad.

It helped that we ran with the old gang: Fred and Jess and Link, Josie and Henry and the Melvin boys. But no more Town Ball and Blindman's Bluff and Circus. They now played a fierce fighting game called War.

They were copying the real war that had broken out in the country. It was the North against the South. Yanks against the Rebels. The kids drew straws to choose sides. Everybody wanted to fight on the side of the North 'cause that was Lincoln's side.

What had set off this real war? I didn't have Old Bob around to explain it to me. But Mr. Roll went to Billy's for his weekly shave and cut. I followed him and met up there with my old friends.

Carlo and Jenny set me straight right off.

The Southern states want to keep using slaves, Carlo explained. *The Northern ones can't abide by it.*

Jenny Lind took over. *So the Southern states broke away from the Northern. My reporter says that Lincoln has found himself fighting a war to keep the states together in one group.*

After all, Carlo said, *that's why they call us a union of states.*

The United States of America, Jenny Lind said.

And Lincoln aims to keep it that way, Carlo said.

From Billy's barbershop to Diller's drugstore,

war was the talk of Springfield. The list of battles fought went on and on: Fort Sumter, Philippi, Big Bethel, Bull Run, Santa Rosa Island, Wilson's Creek, Belmont. . . .

No war can be fought without soldiers. Springfield sent its fair share of young men to fight. The soldiers were seen off in happy parades attended by mothers, sisters, wives, and sweethearts. All too often, the welcome-home parades were much sadder, with muffled drums, weeping ladies, and horse-drawn hearses bearing the bodies of fallen soldiers.

Some people called it Mr. Lincoln's War and cursed him for the loss of these brave young men. But most folks felt it was a war well worth fighting. It was a fight to keep the United States together.

I worried about Lincoln and his troubles. I wondered, did he have a dog to walk and talk with and ease his woes? I took comfort in knowing that at least he still had his sons Willie and Tad.

The boys in the gang jawed about the Washington adventures of their two old pals. The White House, they said, was huge—bigger than any building in Springfield. Their lucky friends had a vast attic to play in, with secret passageways. There were gardens and a fountain. At parties called banquets, they ate giant layer cakes shaped like beehives decorated with spun-sugar bees.

As sons of the president, Willie and Tad got gifts from all over the world. Willie had even gotten his own pony! He rode it on the White House lawn every day, rain or shine. Maybe because he'd ridden his pony in the cold rain, Willie came down with a bad cold. And so did Tad. Their colds turned to fever.

Newspapermen wrote stories about the boys' illness. The doctors said that Tad was expected to die, Willie to live. People in the streets stopped to discuss it in worried voices. Johnny and Frankie fretted.

It turned out those doctors were wrong on both counts. Tad survived the fever. Willie did not.

The evening we got the news, I sat on the horsehair couch with my nose resting on Johnny's lap. Johnny wept. I licked the salty tears from his face and tried not to let on that my own heart was breaking.

But if we were sad, what about Lincoln? That boy had been the light of his pa's life. Gentle, kind-hearted Lincoln, who had saved so many animals from a dire fate, had been powerless to rescue his own perfect boy.

10

THE LAST PARADE

The war raged on. In Washington, they said, Lincoln set aside his grief and went on serving as the president of a United States at war with itself.

In Springfield, the children once more took up their games. Like dogs, they managed to find something good in life. Together, we went fishing. We played War. We watched parades both happy and sad. In the slow blink of an eye, nearly two years passed. I was now a dog of seven years, but there were days when I felt like I was a hundred.

One July day, I was outside the barbershop with Carlo and Jenny. It was devilish hot. We were lying on the sidewalk with our tongues hanging out, wishing that Billy would spring for an awning.

Suddenly, firecrackers started going off. The streets filled with happy, cheering people, dancing and hugging and pounding each other's backs. I knew the signs all too well. It had been a long time since I'd seen happy faces. It seemed like the town was working itself up for a big celebration.

Sorry, friends, but I'm leaving before it gets even noisier around here, I said to Carlos and Jenny Lind.

Please don't go, said Jenny. *This is a great day. The North won an important battle this week in Vicksburg. Many of our boys were there. And we won a second in Gettysburg. My man said that the tide of war is turning in favor of the North.*

Lincoln could use some good news, said Carlo.

That poor man has the weight of the world on his shoulders, Jenny said with a sigh.

Right now I'm worried about the weight of fire-crackers on my poor ears, I said as I headed home to the safety of my couch.

Later, in that fall of 1863, Johnny and Frankie were belly-down on the floor, shooting marbles. Mr. Roll was sitting in his chair, reading the newspaper. I was on my couch, relaxing on my back with my paws in the air. Suddenly, Mr. Roll broke the silence in a voice so eager, I rolled over and perked up my ears.

He was reading from the newspaper. "Listen to this, boys. Mr. Lincoln gave a speech at the dedication of a soldiers' cemetery on the battlefield in Gettysburg. Would you like to hear it?"

The boys sat up to listen:

" 'Four score and seven years ago our fathers brought forth upon this continent, a new nation, conceived in liberty, and dedicated to the proposition that all men are created equal.

" 'Now we are engaged in a great civil war, testing whether that nation, or any nation so conceived, and so dedicated, can long endure. We are met on a great battlefield of that war. We have come to dedicate a portion of that field, as a final resting place for those who here, gave their lives that that nation might live. It is altogether fitting and proper that we should do this.

" 'But in a larger sense, we cannot dedicate—we cannot consecrate—we cannot hallow—this ground. The brave men, living and dead, who struggled here, have consecrated it far above our poor power to add or detract. The world will little

note, nor long remember, what we say here, but it can never forget what they did here. It is for us, the living, rather, to be dedicated here to the unfinished work which they who fought here, have, thus far, so nobly advanced. It is rather for us to be here dedicated to the great task remaining before us— that from these honored dead we take increased devotion to that cause for which they here gave the last full measure of devotion—that we here highly resolve that these dead shall not have died in vain—that this nation, under God, shall have a new birth of freedom—and that government of the people, by the people, for the people, shall not perish from the earth.'"

Mr. Roll said, "Now, *that,* my boys, is what we call a fine speech."

The boys flopped onto their bellies and got back to their marbles. But to my flea-bitten ears, this had the ring of speechifying at its very finest.

The war continued—but now there was hope. The North was winning. In the fall of 1864, Lincoln was reelected. There was cheering on the streets of Springfield, but lucky for me, it wasn't as loud or as happy as when he had won the first time.

The following March, Lincoln's second inauguration party was held. This, too, was a quieter shindig. Maybe, with so many young men off at war, no one felt like celebrating. When the gang played War now, the game nearly always ended with the South surrendering to the North.

So it was no surprise when, a month later on April 9, 1865, the South surrendered to the North for real and true. The War Between the States was over. People marched through the streets and cheered. There was so much celebrating that I took up nearly permanent residence beneath the couch. A week later, I was still under the couch the day Mrs. Roll set up such a howling and wailing that my guts turned to pudding.

What in the world was wrong with her?

I peered out. The family was gathered together in the front hall. They held each other and wept. Sensing they needed me, I joined them.

Johnny knelt and buried his head in my ruff. "Your master's gone, Fido."

I knew my master was gone. He had gone off to Washington and been there for four long years. For the love of dog, why were they crying about it now?

I let them hold me and rock me like I was the one who needed the comforting. I licked their faces till my tongue was sore. When the weeping went on all day and into the night, I crept back beneath the couch.

The next day, Mr. Roll said to his sons, "Clean up Fido real good. We've got a date downtown."

The sight of Johnny holding my brush brought

me out into the open. I like a good brushing.

Afterward, Mr. Roll inspected me. "Very good work, John," he said. "The Lincoln Dog's got to look his best today. Mr. Ingmire is expecting us, and we can't keep him waiting."

"Do we *have* to go?" Johnny whined.

"Fido isn't going to like it," Frankie warned.

"We have to capture Fido's image for the ages," Mr. Roll said.

Downtown, the streets were filled with people talking in low voices. Some of them wept or held hankies to their faces.

Mr. Roll led me past them into a building I'd never been in before. When I sat down hard at the foot of the stairs, Mr. Roll said in an eager voice, "Come, Fido. Come up with us."

I got up and followed them. At the top of the stairs was a big room with windows in the ceiling.

One whiff and I wanted out. I smelled hair oil, dust, *poison.*

Mr. Roll sensed I had come down with a case of the whim-whams. He patted me. "Easy, Fido."

Easy? Easy for him to say.

"Welcome, all," said a strange man in a dark suit with a stiff collar. "Did you bathe the dog?"

"We did not," said Mr. Roll. "He hates baths, and we didn't have the heart. But we brushed him up real good."

"Onward, then," the man said, with a brisk clap of his hands that startled me. "I thought I would pose him here. Lift him up, please."

Mr. Roll boosted me and placed me on a table draped with a piece of fancy cloth.

I gave him worried eyes. *What's all this? I'm not supposed to be on the furniture.*

"He doesn't like it up there, Pa," said Johnny.

"The table's too high up. *Look!* He's shivering."

"He's afeared he'll fall," said Frankie.

"He's afeared of the camera, too," said Johnny.

I was afeared, all right.

"Afraid or not, he's going to have to hold still for the portrait," said the stranger. "If he moves a muscle, it will blur the image and ruin the effect. And we wouldn't want that, would we, boys?"

I looked at the boys and whimpered. *Please can't I just go home?*

Johnny flung his arms around me. Frankie smoothed my fur. "It's okay, old feller," they whispered to me. "You can do this. We know you can."

Gradually, I calmed down. Nothing like the touch of a good boy or two to make a dog settle down right fast.

"Pa," Johnny said, "do you think Frankie and me could just hide behind the table and keep a hand on him? We wouldn't show up in the photo or nothing. Promise."

"It'll keep him calm," Frankie said.

Mr. Roll smiled. "That's using your noggins, boys. You do that. Mr. Ingmire will take the portrait and we'll be out of here in no time at all."

The boys got behind the table. I felt their small, warm hands on my side and haunch.

The stranger squinted hard at me. "I don't think we want him standing," he said. "Sitting or lying would be preferable."

"You heard the man," Johnny whispered. "Lie down like a good dog."

"Lie down and stay," said Frankie as he pressed down gently on my back.

I lowered myself down on the table. I would lie down and stay, but I didn't have to like it. I put my nose on my paws and heaved a loud sigh.

"Good boy, Fido." Frankie stroked my leg.

There was a box not far from the table. It stood on three sticks and was covered with a dark cloth. The man stuck his head beneath the cloth.

After a bit, he lifted his head and frowned at me. "Can't you make him look a little more jolly? I know it's a sad day, but I'd so much rather see a happy dog." He snapped his fingers. I looked lively.

A puff of evil-smelling stink rose from the box. That stink got up my nose. The boys held me while I shook my head and sneezed.

"Boys, keep him where he is. I'll need to take a few more, just in case!" The man held up his hand. "Bear with me a moment or two longer, please, while I prepare the new plate."

A month of Sundays must have passed as the man fidgeted and fumbled.

"That's a brave dog," Frankie told me.

"Mr. Lincoln would be proud of you," Johnny said.

The longer the man fiddled, the more my fear turned to boredom. I had had enough of this room and its foul odors. I had had enough of the fussy man.

Afterward, on the way home, Mr. Roll treated me to a soup bone from my old friend the butcher. I couldn't wait to take it home.

"Tell me again, Pa, why we had to put Fido through all that?" Johnny asked.

"You see, boys," Mr. Roll explained, "as of now, everything Lincoln ever owned or touched has turned to gold. It's an opportunity I'd be a fool to pass up. Ask yourselves, what could be more valuable than Lincoln's dog? An official portrait of that dog! I'm going to have lots of copies printed up. I work hard at carpentering. But there's never enough money. From now on, you boys and your ma will never want for anything."

Later that day, when I was busy with my bone, Johnny once again came calling.

What now? I sighed. Couldn't they all just let a dog gnaw in peace?

"Sorry, boy. They want to see you at the old place," he said to me.

We took the familiar path down the block to the house. It looked different today. It was draped with scary black cloth. This time, the strangers who lived there didn't shoo me away. They opened the front door wide and welcomed me. I wasn't sure I trusted them and their black cloth.

"Come on, Fido," Johnny said, tugging at my collar. "Folks need to lay eyes on you."

I entered the house and shrank back. The rooms were the same, but the furniture was different and the place was crammed with strangers. I saw more sad faces than I'd ever seen in one place. People were sniffling and crying. The place stank of misery. Misery and meat.

"There he is," I heard them whisper in awed voices, "the Lincoln Dog."

Strange hands reached out. Some patted my head and smoothed my coat. Others came at me with scissors, snip-snipping. I shrank from the feel of the cold metal on my skin. They were cutting off pieces of my fur! Was this why I had been brought here? So these folks could shear me like a spring sheep?

"Sorry, boy," Johnny said.

More people came squeezing through the front door, adding to the crowd. I whimpered and scratched at Johnny's leg. *Get me out of here.*

Finally, he understood. "Come on, boy. Let's git before they snatch you bald."

We slipped out the front door. I saw Old Bob standing at the curb with folks gathered around him. I had seen Bob not so long ago. He had been marching in the parade to celebrate the end of the war. Was he ever a sight for sore eyes!

I nosed my way over to Bob's side.

If it isn't Fido, the faithful one, Old Bob hailed me. *Glad to see you've got young Johnny with you. A fine boy, and that's a fact. Reminds me a bit of Willie, God rest his soul.*

What in the world is going on? I asked.

I'm not sure, Old Bob said. *Nobody tells me anything these days. But this morning, John Flynn brought me out of my stall and brushed me till my coat shone. Then he led me here, back to my old stomping grounds and—ouch! There they go again! Quit it!*

Old Bob kicked out sharply with his hind hoof.

A man laughed as he dodged the kick. "I got it!" he shouted, holding up a fistful of wisps. "I got me a genuine piece of Abe's horse's tail."

Old Bob snorted. *A couple of gents from out of town offered John Flynn a small fortune for me. Can you imagine anyone paying for an old swayback like me? Those men must have been plumb crazy.*

They were snipping my fur inside the house, I said.

Old Bob said, *Even if they snipped you bald, your fur would grow back. I've only got so much hair left, and my tail grows sparser by the day. I need this tail to swat flies!*

What I want to know, I said, *is where in the world did all these people come from? Why are they so sad?*

I wonder . . . , said Old Bob, licking his lips thoughtfully. *You don't suppose, do you . . . ?*

Spit it out, my friend! I said.

Well, far be it from me to get a dog's hopes up. But do you suppose he might finally be coming home?

Who? I asked.

Why, Lincoln, of course. Who else?

For a brief moment, my heart surged. Then hope drained away like water from a cracked jug. *Nah,* I said. *If Lincoln were really coming home, there'd be brass bands marching down the street. There'd be cannons booming and banners waving, and everyone everywhere you looked would be busting with happiness. Look around you, old feller. Do you see a single joyful face?*

Old Bob shook himself out, nose to tail. *Nope. It was a stupid idea. Must be getting old and foolish.*

It was a nice thought, though, I said wistfully. *An awful nice thought.*

One day soon after, I awoke to the sound of muffled drums coming from over at the Chicago & Alton depot, west of the town square. It must be time to welcome home more fallen soldiers. So *that* was the reason for all this sadness!

"Come on, Fido. It's time to go," Johnny said.

Johnny looked different today. He was wearing a little black suit and a stiff collar and his hair was wet and fresh combed. He was in his Sunday-go-to-meeting duds. But it wasn't Sunday.

Outside there were people lining the street as far as I could see.

"Hurry up, Fido," Johnny said.

Dodging the crowd, we cut through backyards until we came to the old house on the corner. Even more people filled the front and side yards. Johnny and me wormed our way toward the sidewalk until we were standing right out in front.

The muffled drums were louder. All of a sudden, the biggest hearse I'd ever seen rolled into sight. It was pulled slowly by six black horses wearing long black plumes on their heads. Folks flung out their arms as it came on. They wept and moaned and blew their noses into their hankies. I looked around at all the tearstained faces. Just how many dead soldiers did this one hearse hold that so many people had come out to weep and wail?

The hearse rumbled past. Following in its wake came Old Bob, his swayback draped in a plain black mourning blanket. I barked out a greeting. Old Bob picked up his sorrowful head and whinnied. *I was right, Fido. And how I wish I wasn't.*

What's that you say, Bob? I struggled to hear him over the mourners.

Lincoln has finally come home to us, Bob said. *Only he's come home in a box.*

I looked at the long flower-draped box in the back of the hearse. I tell you, my yaller fur stood on end, because I finally understood. The long black box held Lincoln, the man who had always shown me such kindness. The man who smelled like no other: like timber and woodsmoke and river and milk and barn and great sadness.

Deep down inside me, something broke. I

threw back my head and bawled to high heaven.

Folks looked at me. I heard them murmur, "The Lincoln Dog. He *knows.*"

Just like Old Bob said, Lincoln was finally coming home, to the town where he had known happiness and love and the best of times—where Eddy lay waiting for him. My man had come home to me, just as I had always known he would.

APPENDIX

The Animal Lover

Almost everyone agrees that Abraham Lincoln was one of the greatest U.S. presidents. During the darkest hours of the Civil War, he played a vital role in preserving the Union. While the war between North and South still raged, on January 1, 1863, he issued the Emancipation Proclamation. It stated "that all persons held as slaves" in the rebel territory "are and henceforward shall be free." And so began the process that would eventually end slavery.

Lincoln had respect and sympathy for his fellow man. But not everyone knows that Lincoln's respect for life extended beyond humans to all creatures, great and small.

Abraham Lincoln was a big animal lover!

Young Abe got his first pet when he was six years old and living in a log cabin on a Kentucky farm. A neighbor gave Lincoln a piglet, which he carried home in the hem of his shirt. "That pig," Lincoln would say as an adult, "was my companion. I played with him, and taught him tricks. We used to play hide-and-seek. I can see his little face now, peeking around the corner of the house. . . ." The pig kept growing until, one day, Abe's father told him the time had come to butcher it for meat. Abe was so sad.

At the age of seven, Abe witnessed a stray dog being kicked. Abe was too small to stop the man, but he hollered loud enough to drive the man off. Lincoln nursed the dog, named Honey, back to health. Perhaps to make up for the lost pig, his parents let him keep the dog.

The Lincoln family moved to Indiana, near the Little Pigeon Creek, in 1816. He and his sister rarely went to school, but for the subject of an at-home composition, he chose cruelty to animals. The boy who would grow up to write some of the most eloquent presidential speeches also got early practice standing on tree stumps, holding forth on the subject of animal protection.

Cruelty to animals was commonplace on the frontier. Dogs, cats, horses, mules, and even chipmunks were regularly mistreated. Abe once took the local boys to task for tormenting a turtle by putting hot coals on it to force it out of its shell. He said to them, "An ant's life is to it as sweet as ours to us."

It probably comes as no surprise that when Abe

grew up and had a family of his own, there were pets aplenty, both before and during the White House years. As William Herndon, Lincoln's law partner, once said, if Mr. Lincoln's children "wanted a dog—cat—rat" or anything else in the animal kingdom, "it was all right and well treated—housed—petted—fed—fondled."

At various times, they had cats, dogs, horses, ponies, cows, goats, turkeys, turtles, rabbits, and snakes. When Mrs. Lincoln was asked what her husband's hobby was, she said, "Cats." Lincoln relieved stress by stroking a cat and listening to it purr.

Cats probably had it a little better than dogs back then. They got rid of vermin, which was considered useful. But a dog that couldn't hunt, herd, or guard was spurned as a pest. The streets and alleys of towns and cities across the nation teemed with hungry, diseased, and abused dogs. Nobody wanted these tramps, as they were called. People feared that they carried rabies. In those pre-vaccine days, people like Mary Lincoln lived in dread of rabies.

When Robert Lincoln was bitten by a dog, she feared he had contracted the deadly disease. Lincoln took the child to Terre Haute, Indiana, where a locally famous practitioner used a "mad stone" to "cure" Robert of the disease. A popular folk remedy at the time, the "mad stone" was actually a hardened hair ball from the stomach of a cow or deer! Wisdom had it that the mad stone, when rubbed over a bite, would pull out the poison.

Luckily for Fido, Lincoln had a weakness for tramps. We don't know exactly how Fido came to be the family dog, but it's a good bet that Lincoln rescued him as a stray. Fido was a mixed breed and, according to Lincoln's oldest son, Robert, not much to look at. Nevertheless, Fido quickly won over his adoptive family, and it was not long before he had the run of the house. For five happy years, he came and went as he pleased. He drove the house-proud Mary Lincoln wild by leaving muddy paw prints on her rugs and drapes. He dined upon scraps from the table and slept on a horsehair couch in the parlor.

With the presidential election of 1860, Fido's comfortable life with the Lincolns drew to an end. The loud noises that came with Lincoln's fame and victory—shouting, firecrackers, cannon fire, train whistles, big brass bands—ruined Fido's peace of mind. Today, a veterinarian would probably have diagnosed him as having noise phobia. No one knows yet what causes it or whether its origins are physical or mental. Nevertheless, it is a real syndrome suffered by some dogs that are super-sensitive to loud noises—thunderstorms and firecrackers, especially. They can even be jolted by harmless-seeming sounds like doors creaking or hands clapping. Their immediate reaction is to panic and do anything they can to get away from the noise. Often, they seek shelter and hide.

By observing Fido, Lincoln saw that noise and excitement made his dog edgy and miserable. Understanding that life in Washington would offer only more of the same, Lincoln opted to leave Fido (and his favorite horsehair couch) in Springfield in the care of a friend and neighbor, a carpenter named John Roll. Roll had two sons, John and Frank, who were friends with Willie and Tad. Fido knew them and trusted them, which probably eased the transition.

Upon Lincoln's departure for Washington, he

left a letter for Roll. In it, he set forth in no un-certain terms the rules of Fido's care. Fido must be allowed to run free and never be tied up. He was not to be scolded for tracking mud into the house. He was to be treated to scraps from the family table. Fido being a famous dog by then, Roll must have been mindful of the privilege of being entrusted with the Lincoln Dog and the importance of abid-ing by these rules. Following Lincoln's death, Roll was probably also aware of the potential monetary advantages.

It's not known when exactly Fido sat for his his-toric studio photograph. John Roll probably com-missioned it soon after Lincoln's death. The dog's image was quickly mass-produced on calling cards, which are now rare collector's items. Roll also owned a door that he had replaced from the Lin-coln home. (Who knows, maybe Lincoln had had it replaced because it was damaged by Fido's claw marks!) In any event, Roll wound up selling it for a good deal of money. Everything that Lincoln ever owned, saw, or touched increased immeasurably in value after April 15, 1865, when the president died the day after being shot by John Wilkes Booth in Ford's Theatre in Washington, D.C.

Following a period of lying in state in Washington, Lincoln's body—along with Willie's—was brought home to Springfield in a nine-car private train. It was accompanied by statesmen, friends, and, for part of the way, Lincoln's oldest son, Robert. Mrs. Lincoln was too upset to travel and remained in the White House with Tad.

The population of Springfield swelled from 15,000 to 100,000 on the day of the funeral. Fido was among the vast crowd of mourners who stood and watched the hearse roll through the streets, going out of its way to pass the old house on the corner. Father and son were first buried in the public receiving vault in Oak Ridge Cemetery. Eddy's body was later moved from Hutchinson Cemetery to Oak Ridge to join his father and brother in a small family vault.

Much of what we know about Fido comes from Dorothy Kunhardt, the author of the book *Pat the Bunny.* Her father, Frederick Meserve, had one of the largest collections of Lincoln memorabilia in the world. She grew up surrounded by these fascinating objects and documents. She met "little Johnnie Roll" when he was over 90, and in 1954 wrote an article for *Life* magazine titled "Lincoln's Lost Dog."

But was Fido ever really lost? Not really. After all, he was the Lincoln Dog. And over the years, thanks to his enduring fame, Fido has become as common a name for dogs as Spot or Rex.

To learn more about Abraham Lincoln, visit:

- illinois.gov/alplm
- underhishat.alplm.org

To see photographs and take a virtual tour of the Lincolns' Springfield home, visit:

- nps.gov/liho

To find out more about Fido, as well as Lincoln's animal-friendly White House, visit:

- presidentialpetmuseum.com

The Case Against Cruelty

Thomas Paine—one of the heroes of the American Revolution—took a strong stand against cruelty to animals. In *The Age of Reason,* published in 1794, he wrote, "Everything of persecution and revenge between man and man, and everything of cruelty to animals, is a violation of moral duty" and "the only idea we can have of serving God is that of contributing to the happiness of the living creation God has made."

Although there have been laws in this country guarding against cruelty to animals since the time of the *Mayflower* settlers, most of the early ones were weak and difficult to enforce. Typical of them was a New York law of 1829 that was limited to animals considered as commercial property, like horses and cattle. It covered only violence done by individuals to *other people's property,* which implied that it was perfectly legal to harm one's own animals. The law also said that the harm had to have *malicious* intent, something difficult to prove in a court of law. Lastly, the punishment was a small fine—a sure sign that the law lacked teeth.

In Lincoln's home state of Illinois, in the 1850s

and '60s, there was little legal protection for dogs. Strays—known as tramps—were seen as a menace to public health. Police were authorized to keep the canine population down. During regular "cullings" in many towns and cities, strays could be shot on sight. Bounties were even offered, awarding so many pennies per head. Lincoln was quick to put a collar on Fido probably because dogs wearing collars were spared by cullers and bounty hunters.

One person, in particular, was outraged by these cullings. In 1841, an abolitionist and advocate for the rights of women and Native Americans named Lydia Maria Child likened culling in the streets of New York City to the bloodshed in Paris during the Reign of Terror of the French Revolution. She believed that culling was cruel, and that violence against animals led, more often than not, to violence against humans. She also felt that humans could learn to be kinder to one another if they were encouraged to be kinder to animals.

Another early champion of animal rights was American shipping heir Henry Bergh. He believed that "mercy to animals means mercy to mankind." In 1865, Bergh traveled to England and observed the doings of the Royal Society for the Protection of Animals. When he came home, he asked the New York legislature for a charter to start a new organization. Modeled after the British, its purpose was "to provide effective means for the prevention of cruelty to animals throughout the United States, to enforce all laws which are now, or may hereafter be, enacted for the protection of animals, and to secure, by lawful means, the arrest and conviction of all persons violating such laws." That is how the American Society for the Prevention of Cruelty to Animals came to be.

As its first president, Bergh set out to change and strengthen the existing laws—those that covered animals considered commercial property. His main focus was on cart horses and mules, among the most abused animals of the day. It was common practice to work an animal nearly to death and then to abandon it on the streets. The New York Act of 1866 stated: "Every owner, driver or possessor of an old, maimed or diseased horse or mule, turned loose or left disabled in any street . . . for more than three hours . . . shall . . . be adjudged guilty of a misdemeanor."

The New York Act of 1867 took another major step forward, broadening its scope to include not just commercial animals, but "any living creature." Moreover, it outlawed the practice of animal fighting: bull, bear, cock, and dog. It authorized the ASPCA to impound stray animals (giving rise to the term *dog pound*) and offer them "sufficient quantity of good and wholesome food and water." It permitted anyone, including ASPCA officers, to enter a private home and care for a neglected or abused animal's needs. And it empowered those officers to arrest violators of the law. If convicted, the guilty were subject to high fines.

Henry Bergh was a true pioneer in the field of animal rights reform. At the time of his death in 1888, thirty-seven of the existing thirty-eight states had passed anticruelty laws. Today, his organization is one of the largest not-for-profit humane societies in the world, with over one million members. Bergh's society also gave rise to the formation of thousands of other similar societies. Individual, independent SPCA groups now operate in every state, concerned with animal cruelty, shelter, and adoption but also with humane education, poison control, and assisted therapy.

We have come a long way toward making the world a safer and kinder place for animals. But many people continue to fight for stricter laws against puppy mills and medical experimentation, as well as harsher sentences for abusers.

For an excellent overview of the history of animal cruelty and the humane movement, visit:

- learningtogive.org/resources/animal-cruelty

To learn more about Henry Bergh and the ASPCA, visit:

- aspca.org/about-us/history-of-the-aspca

In Praise of Mixed Breeds

When you look at the photograph of Fido, what do you see? A retriever? A hound? A bit of basset in the ears and jowls, perhaps? You may see aspects of all three—and many more—because Fido was a mutt, or mixed breed.

Belonging to no one single breed, a mutt is often a mixture of dozens of different breeds—which ones being anyone's guess. A person wanting to get a dog must decide: *Should I get a purebred or a mixed breed?*

There is something to be said in favor of getting a purebred. It involves less guesswork. But this advantage doesn't come cheap. The cost of buying a dog from a reputable breeder varies depending upon the breed, anywhere from two thousand dollars for, say, a golden retriever, to nearly two million dollars for a Tibetan mastiff. This arrangement allows you to know the dog's parents. It also lets you know, more or less, what you are getting. Purebred dogs have been bred to conform to an ideal profile, both physically and in terms of behavior.

For instance, a beagle is a scent hound, a Labrador retriever is a water dog, a shih tzu is a lapdog. Depending on what someone is looking for in a dog, these are all desirable traits. On the negative side, a beagle will follow its nose right out of your yard, a Lab's oily coat can have a strong doggie smell, and a shih tzu's flat face puts it at risk of heatstroke.

Buying a mixed breed is more a matter of potluck. Think of mutts as being the canine equivalent of America's "great melting pot." The same thing that makes America great makes mutts great. Some people say that because their genetic background is so varied, mixed-breed dogs are less likely to suffer from inherited physical ailments and extreme behaviors. New studies, however, show that mixed breeds don't necessarily have a genetic advantage. It all depends upon the disorder. For example, heart conditions occur more frequently in purebreds, but mixed breeds suffer more knee ligament problems. Whatever the science may be, one thing is certain: a mutt is like a fur-wrapped surprise package on four legs. And maybe that's why mutts are the most popular dogs in America.

If getting a mutt is your preference, make sure you adopt a happy, healthy dog with a good temperament. Do your research. Find out what brought the dog to the institution. Does it have medical problems? A history of abuse? Is the dog friendly and relaxed or shy and fearful? A good way to hedge your bet is to adopt an adult dog rather than a puppy. His or her character and temperament will be fully formed, and you'll know exactly what you're getting. (One important thing you will probably *not* get is a dog that needs to be house-broken!)

Shelters and humane societies across the country are overflowing with mutts of all ages, shapes, and sizes that need good homes—and the cost will be reasonable, usually in the form of a donation to the institution. Even if you are looking for a purebred, about 25 percent of dogs in shelters *are* purebred. If you're thinking of adopting, visit:

- humanesociety.org/animals/dogs/tips /choosing_dog.html

  To find an animal shelter near you, go to:
- theshelterpetproject.org/pet-search

Fido (above and below)

The Reverend Brown and Old Bob

Willie and Tad Lincoln with their cousin
Lockwood Todd

Tad Lincoln

Willie Lincoln